ANDERSON

T5-AQQ-636

*Inside the NFL*

# THE
# NEW YORK
# GIANTS

## BOB ITALIA
### ABDO & Daughters

Published by Abdo & Daughters, 4940 Viking Drive, Suite 622, Edina, Minnesota 55435.

Copyright © 1996 by Abdo Consulting Group, Inc., Pentagon Tower, P.O. Box 36036, Minneapolis, Minnesota 55435 USA. International copyrights reserved in all countries. No part of this book may be reproduced in any form without written permission from the publisher.

Printed in the United States.

Cover Photo credits: Wide World Photos / Allsport
Interior Photo credits: Allsport, page 27
                        Bettmann Photos, pages 4, 5, 7, 10, 11, 14, 15, 18-20, 22, 25
                        Wide World Photos, pages 8, 9, 12, 13, 16, 18, 19


Edited by Kal Gronvall

## Library of Congress Cataloging-in-Publication data

Italia, Bob, 1955—
    New York Giants / Bob Italia
    p.    cm.    --    (Inside the NFL)
    Includes Index.
    Summary: A brief history of the New York Giants, one of the oldest continuing teams in the National Football League.
    ISBN 1-56239-457-6
    1. New York Giants (Football team)--Juvenile literature. [1. New York Giants (Football team)] I. Title. II. Series: Italia, Bob, 1955— Inside the NFL.
    GV956.N4I83        1995
    796.332'64'097471--dc20            95-883
                                 CIP
                                 AC

# CONTENTS

# A Deep Football Tradition

The New York Giants have a deep football tradition. As one of the original NFL teams, the Giants have seen many great players come and go—players like Steve Owen, Arnie Hebner, Emlen Tunnell, Mel Hein, Frank Gifford, and Sam Huff. Despite their long history, the Giants have not experienced much success until lately. Players like Phil Simms and Lawrence Taylor helped make the Giants Super Bowl champions twice in five years. The 1986 Giants were considered one of the best teams ever, and were on the verge of a dynasty until injuries and personal problems sidetracked the team.

These days, the Giants are in the midst of rebuilding. Having already attained championship status, the Giants know what it takes to reach the top of the NFL.

**Frank Gifford, playing for the USC Trojans, went on to run for the New York Giants.**

**Phil Simms helped make the Giants Super Bowl champions.**

# A Giant Beginning

The Giants first owner, Tim Mara, bought the team in 1925. In those days, the game was played differently. The athletes played offense and defense. The games were low-scoring, and few passes were thrown. Equipment consisted of leather helmets and hightop shoes. Sometimes teams played four games in eight days, and fans paid a dollar to watch the game at a stadium. Players made fifty dollars per contest.

In the 1920s, the Giants had losing seasons. They had three coaches in three years. Then, in 1927, Earl Potteiger led the Giants to an 11-1-1 record.

Potteiger left in 1930. Steve Owen, one of the Giants' players, was willing to coach and play. Owen believed that a good defense would win championships. He formed a new defensive alignment called the "umbrella" defense that featured a six-man front, one linebacker, and four defensive backs. When the opposing quarterback dropped back to pass, two defensive lineman dropped back to form an umbrella-shaped semicircle. Owen's approach worked so well, Mara gave him a long-term contract. Owen would coach the Giants for the next 23 seasons.

In 1953, Owen retired after leading the Giants to six divisional titles and two league championships. His 150-100-17 career record remains one of the NFL's best.

Many great athletes played during Owen's long career—Hall of Fame players like quarterback Arnie Herber, defensive back Emlen Tunnell and center Mel Hein. Eventually, Owen too was named to the Hall of Fame.

# Howell and Gifford

Jim Lee Howell became the Giants' head coach in 1954. Howell chose assistants who could motivate football players. Vince Lombardi, Tom Landry, Dick Nolan, and Alex Webster all worked under Howell, and would one day become successful NFL head coaches.

To be successful, Howell also needed good football players—and he made sure he got them. One such player was Frank Gifford. Gifford, a great running back from the University of Southern California, had an outstanding professional career. He was also a team leader who imparted a winning attitude on his teammates.

In 12 seasons, Gifford led the Giants to five division titles—all the while scoring a team-record 78 touchdowns. In 1956, Gifford scored the touchdown that beat the Chicago Bears in the NFL championship game.

**Some of the Giants front line, 1935.**

# The Best Game Ever?

On December 28, 1958, the Giants played the Baltimore Colts in one of his biggest championship games in NFL history. The game became known as the Yankee Stadium Classic—and it would change the fortunes of the NFL forever.

The Giants were led by quarterback Charlie Conerly. The Colts had Johnny Unitas, who often threw to Raymond Berry and Lenny Moore.

On game day, the rains came and muddied the field. Each team had many fumbles, interceptions, and missed field goals. Despite the sloppy play, the game's outcome wouldn't be decided until the very end.

**On December 28, 1958, the Giants played the Baltimore Colts for the NFL championship. The Colts won in overtime.**

**Frank Gifford (16), halfback for the New York Giants, runs past the Colts' defense.**

With three minutes remaining, the Giants led 17-14. But then Johnny Unitas drove the Colts 73 yards. The Giants defense stiffened, and the drive stalled. Baltimore settled for a Lou Michels field goal which sent the game into sudden death overtime.

Baltimore got the ball and began another long drive. On the one-yard-line, the Giants' defense prepared for a pass play. But fullback Alan Ameche burst over the goal line for the game-winning touchdown and a 23-17 championship victory.

After the game, the Giants were down. But Tim Mara was proud of his team. A few weeks later, Mara died. His sons assumed responsibility for the team.

# Yelberton Comes to Town

Though the Giants finished second in 1960, Jim Lee Howell ended his coaching career. The Giants offered Vince Lombardi of the Green Bay Packers the coaching job. When he declined, assistant Allie Sherman was named head coach.

Sherman immediately went to work. He traded Conerly for San Francisco quarterback Y.A. (Yelberton Abraham) Tittle, whom the 49ers felt was too slow to be effective.

In 1961, Tittle led the Giants to a 10-3-1 record. That same year, he was named Most Valuable Player (MVP). Tittle had three more good years with the Giants. He also led the them to three straight conference titles.

Middle linebacker Sam Huff was also a popular player. His ferocious tackles brought much attention to the linebacking position. Huff came up with some of football's most well-known defensive terms, like "red dog," "blitz," and "sack."

**Y. A. Tittle.**

# A Giant Fall

In 1964, Sam Huff was sent to the Washington Redskins. In 1965, Y.A. Tittle retired. Immediately, the Giants began to slide. Finding new, talented players to replace the old stars was not easy. In 1964, the Giants fell to 2-12.

During the next 15 years, the Giants had five different head coaches. They also had some great quarterbacks. Earl Morrall, Fran Tarkenton, Norm Snead, and Craig Morton all played for New York. But the Giants needed more than one star player. To win championships, the Giants had to rebuild their defense.

**Sam Huff in his Washington Redskins uniform.**

During this rebuilding period, New York also changed stadiums. The Giants played at the Polo Grounds, Yankee Stadium, and at Yale University. But their record never improved.

The breaking point came during a game in November 1978 against Philadelphia. Leading 17-12 over the Eagles with 28 seconds remaining in the game, the Giants held the ball on their 29-yard line. All the Giants quarterback had to do was take one final snap, fall on the ball, and run out the clock. But New York's offensive coach sent in a running play. Quarterback Joe Pisarcik took the snap, turned—and stuck the ball into fullback Larry Csonka's hip. Czonka knocked the ball from Pisarcik's hands, and it fell to the frozen field. Eagles defender Herman Edwards picked up the ball and ran for the winning touchdown. Management was furious. It was time for a change.

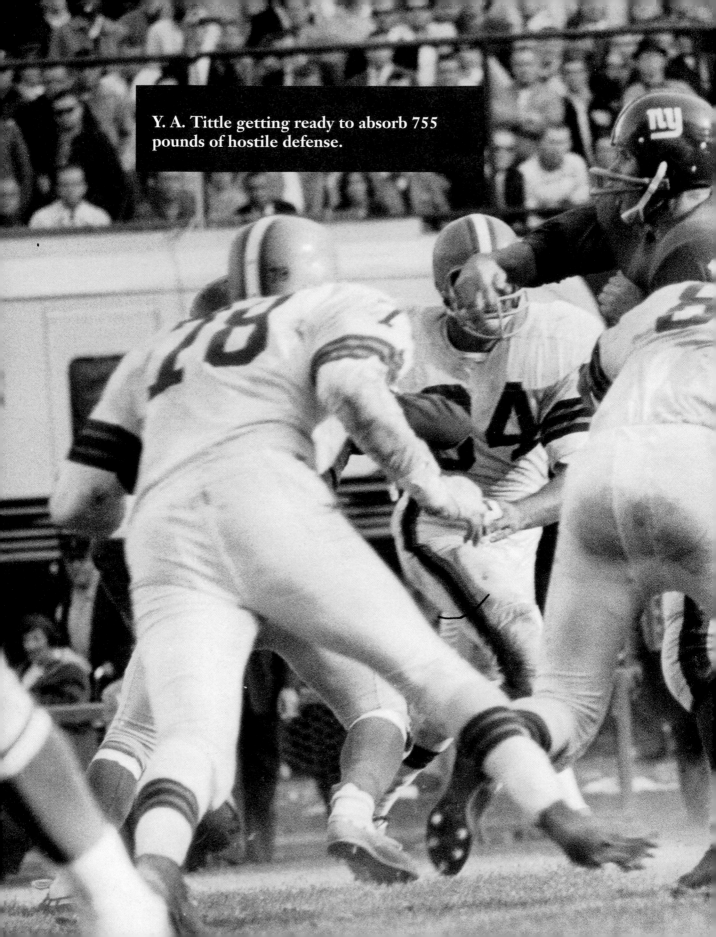

Y. A. Tittle getting ready to absorb 755 pounds of hostile defense.

# A New Beginning

In 1979, George Young became the Giants' new general manager. Over the next decade, he would slowly rebuild New York into a championship team. But first, Young needed a head coach and a quarterback.

**Quarterback Phil Simms.**

The Giants chose Ray Perkins from the San Diego Chargers. Then, in the 1981 college draft, New York selected quarterback Phil Simms from Morehead State College as their first-round pick.

Immediately, New York fans criticized the selection. Simms had played for a small school and was not well-known. But Simms had a strong arm and a winning attitude. He wanted to prove the critics wrong.

To make sure Simms succeeded, New York surrounded him with talented offensive players. The New York offense improved, and the critics fell silent.

Despite the improvements, New York did not have the kind of defense that could help win championships. In 1980, the Giants had given up 425 points—the second most in the NFL. If New York wanted to reach the playoffs, they needed to build their defense around an impact player.

# L.T.

After the 1982 season, Perkins left the Giants to coach the University of Alabama. New York immediately promoted assistant coach Bill Parcells to head coach. Several weeks later, the Giants drafted linebacker Lawrence Taylor.

**Lawrence Taylor making a tackle.**

Lawrence Taylor, legendary linebacker.

When he was young, Taylor dreamed of a professional baseball career. But after seeing a few NFL games, he became interested in football. Taylor learned that the local Jaycees was forming a football team—and that they were going to play a game in Pittsburgh, Pennsylvania. Taylor signed up. He wanted to see the world.

The Jaycees coach immediately noticed Taylor's size, strength, and quickness. He told Taylor to play linebacker.

Taylor was thrilled, but he had no idea what a linebacker was. He went to his school's library and read about famous linebackers like Green Bay's Ray Nitschke, Pittsburgh's Jack Ham, and New York's Sam Huff. He learned how they became successful— by playing smart and mean.

After he played for the Jaycees, the 5-foot 7-inch, 180-pound Taylor made the Lafeyette High School team. His coach, Melvin Jones, had inspirational sayings plastered all over his office walls. One quote stuck with Taylor: "If you can perceive it and believe it, then you can achieve it."

Eventually, Taylor played for the University of North Carolina (UNC). At 6-foot 3-inches tall and 230 pounds, he was one of the biggest and fastest college linebackers. Taylor could single-handedly change the course—and outcome—of a game. He often came up with a crucial, game-saving tackle, quarterback sack  or even caused a fumble. In his senior year at UNC, one-third of his tackles were behind the line of scrimmage. Most professional scouts thought that Taylor might become an NFL star. Parcells *knew* that Taylor could.

**20** **30** **40** **5**

Bill Morgan, tackle
for the Giants, 1935.

New York
Giants

*New*
*Gic*

Y. A. Tittle quarterbacked
the Giants, 1962.

Frank Gifford joined the
Giants in the 1950s.

**10** **20** **30** **40** **5**

0    40                                20        10

Running back Joe
Morris, 1986.

Giants quarterback Phil
Simms, 1993.

York

ants

New York
Giants

Giants linebacker Lawrence
Taylor, 1980s-90s.

Giants running back
Ottis Anderson, 1990s.

0    40          30        20

# The Parcells Era

By the end of his first year in the NFL, Taylor made the impact Parcells had counted upon. In his rookie season, Taylor had nine-and-a-half sacks, 94 solo tackles, and 39 assists. More importantly, he changed the way the other teams looked at the Giants' defense. He scared them.

Taylor was everywhere on the field. If a team wanted to run or pass against the Giants, they had to deal with L.T. first. With Taylor running the defense and Simms running the offense, the Giants were on their way toward greatness. In 1984, Parcells launched a major housecleaning. The offensive line was revamped in favor of big, powerful athletes who could blow holes in opponents' lines and surround Simms with a wall of protection.

The Giants jumped out to three victories in the first four games. But then an

**Bill Parcells, holding the Super Bowl trophy.**

early autumn slump dropped them to 4-4.  At midseason, the Giants made a run at the playoffs with five wins in six weeks.  They trounced the Redskins and Cowboys back to back and beat the Cardinals two weeks after that.  Losses to the Cardinals and Saints evened their recorded, but the Giants captured an unexpected wild-card spot.

In the playoffs, the Giants beat the L. A. Rams 16-13.  But then New York ran into Joe Montana and the San Francisco 49ers in the second round of the playoffs.  The 49ers won 21-10.  The Giants were disappointed.  But the best was yet to come.

In 1985, the Giants were a team on the rise.  For the second straight year, New York made the playoffs as a wild-card team.  Only a pair of frustrating defeats at the hands of the Cowboys kept the Giants from the NFC East title.  Of the team's six losses, only one was by as many as seven points.

Running back Joe Morris emerged as one of the NFL's top rushers.  In 1985, Morris ran for 1,336 yards and scored 21 touchdowns.  Mark Bavaro proved to be an outstanding tight end.  Simms continued his improvement.  His 3,829 passing yards put him into the Pro Bowl where he was named MVP.

In the first round of the playoffs, the Giants beat San Francisco 17-3.  But then New York lost to eventual Super Bowl champion Chicago 21-0.

# Super Giants

The next year, 1986, did not start as New York's year. Running back Joe Morris held out for contract renegotiation until four hours before the first game. Then the Giants dropped the opener to arch-rival Dallas 31-28. Top wide receiver Lionel Manuel was injured most of the time. Still, the Giants won

**Joe Morris runs past Denver defensemen.**

their next five games before losing to Seattle.  After that, they just kept on winning, rolling to the Eastern Division championship with a 14-2 record.  Eight Giants were named to the Pro Bowl—including Lawrence Taylor, who led the NFL in sacks with 20 1/2 and was named league MVP.  Linebacker Harry Carson started an NFL tradition by dumping a cooler full of Gatorade on Parcells after every New York victory.

In the first round of the playoffs, the Giants thrashed the 49ers 49-3.  It was a sign of things to come.  The next opponent was the Washington Redskins.  In a windy Giants Stadium, New York seized a 17-0 halftime lead, then turned the game over to their smothering defense.  The Redskins could not move the ball.  The Giants were headed to the Super Bowl against John Elway and the Denver Broncos.

The first half was evenly played as Denver took a 10-9 lead.  But the second half belonged to the Giants.  New York took the second-half kickoff and drove to their own 47 where they faced a fourth-and-one.  Instead of punting, the Giants ran a quarterback sneak for two yards and a first down.  New York completed the 63-yard drive with a 13-yard touchdown pass from Simms to Bavaro.  Before the quarter ended, the Giants had built their lead to 26-10. The fourth quarter saw two more New York touchdowns before Denver responded with 10 points.  The Giants went on to win 39-20.

Although Elway passed for 304 yards, the Broncos running game was shut down.  Simms was named MVP, completing 22-of-25 passes for a record 88 percent.  The defensive standout was linebacker Carl Banks who racked up 10 solo tackles.

# A Giant Dynasty?

The Giants were on the verge of a dynasty. But dark clouds were already gathering on the horizon. Taylor suffered from personal problems. Mark Bavaro held out for more money. Harry Carson retired, and various injuries plagued the Giants throughout 1987 and 1988. Parcells needed to retool his team if the Giants were to return to the Super Bowl.

The following year, the Giants put together their second-best won-lost record in 26 years, finishing 12-4. The surprise of the season was Ottis Anderson, who stepped in for the injured Joe Morris and produced the sixth 1,000-yard rushing season of his career. Rookie Dave Meggett was another surprise, making the Pro Bowl with his jitterbug kick returning and long-distance pass-catching. But in the second round of the playoffs, the Giants lost 19-13 to the L.A. Rams. Were the Giants on their way up, or down?

In 1990, the Giants set an NFL record for fewest turnovers with 14—less than one per game. A 10-game winning streak from the opening of the season locked up the division title early.

The huge offensive line, anchored by tackle Jumbo Elliott, opened holes for Ottis Anderson, Dave Meggett, and rookie Rodney Hampton. The Taylor-led defense finished first overall in the NFC. The Giants seemed ready for a run at the Super Bowl.

In the second round of the playoffs, the Giants routed the Bears 31-3 in New York. Backup quarterback Jeff Hostetler, playing for an injured Phil Simms, lit up the scoreboard with his passing and running. Now it was on to San Francisco to play the 49ers.

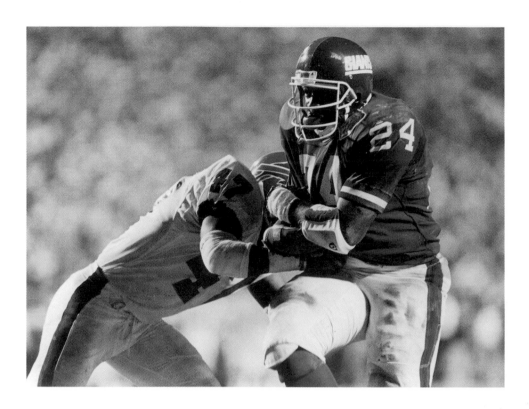

**Giants running back Ottis Anderson runs past a Bills defender.**

The Giants ended the 49ers dreams of a third-straight Super Bowl championship in a game that had seven field goals and only one touchdown. Five of the field goals were kicked by the Giants' Matt Bahr. With Simms still unable to play, the Giants used a conservative ground attack to keep the pressure off Hostetler, who hit on several key passes to help set up the field-goal attempts.

But the game was in doubt until the very end. Trailing 13-9, the Giants surprised the 49ers with a fake punt with Gary Reasons running 30 yards to set up a 38-yard Bahr field goal to bring New York within a point of San Francisco.

The 49ers tried to run out the clock, but Roger Craig fumbled and Taylor recovered with 2:36 left. The Giants drove to within field-goal range on a pair of Hostetler passes. Then, as time ran out, Bahr hit his fifth field goal for the winner.

Super Bowl XXV was the closest one ever, with a one-point margin separating the winning New York Giants from the losing Buffalo Bills. As it happened in the NFC Championship game, the decision came down to the final play of the game.

After Buffalo took a 12-10 halftime lead, the Giants scored on a third-quarter touchdown run by Ottis Anderson. But then the Bills responded with a 31-yard touchdown run on the first play of the fourth quarter.

Down 19-17, the Giants put together their third long, time-consuming drive of the game—74 yards in 14 plays—with Bahr's 21-yard field goal. It gave New York a 20-19 lead.

But Buffalo wasn't finished. In the final two minutes, the Bills drove from their own 10 to the New York 29. But Scott Norwood's attempt for a 47-yard, game-winning field goal sailed wide right. The Giants were Super Bowl champions once again.

When Parcells resigned as head coach in May, everyone knew changes were in store for the defending Super Bowl champions. But nobody thought a .500 record and no playoff berth would be some of the changes. New coach Ray Handley's first decision was to decide the starting quarterback. He chose Jeff Hostetler. But Hostetler was ineffective and was replaced by Simms. Ottis Anderson was finally sent to the bench, and a star was born in the name of Rodney Hampton, who gained 1,059 yards rushing. The Giants defense was still tough, but age was starting to slow the play of Lawrence Taylor, Carl Banks, and other veterans.

# The Youth Movement

Handley lasted just 19 months as Giants head coach. Dan Reeves moved east from Denver to take over. Taylor was planning to retire, but then he suffered a season-ending injury which postponed his retirement.

The one bright spot was Rodney Hampton. Again he was one of the league's top runners with 1,141 yards and 14 touchdowns. Six losses in the final seven games and a season full of turmoil meant more changes in New York as 1993 approached.

In 1993, the Giants were one of the surprise teams, going 11-5 and making the playoffs. Simms had a great comeback, completing 61.8 percent of his passes for 3,038 yards. He also started every game for the first time in seven years. Even more, Rodney Hampton rushed for 1,077 yards.

Following six straight victories, New York was tied atop the division with Dallas at 11-4 going into the final game and looking for a first-round bye in the playoffs. But the Cowboys prevailed 16-13. After the season, Lawrence Taylor finally announced his retirement.

**Rodney Hampton.**

Though Simms had a good year in 1993, the Giants decided not to sign him the following year. Reeves was rebuilding the team with youth, and he signed rookie quarterback Dave Brown.

The Giants started off winning five games in a row, and it seemed the youth movement was working. But then they dropped five straight as Brown's inexperience began to show. The Giants salvaged the season with a final-game victory over the Cowboys. But the win did not get them into the playoffs.

§

Dan Reeves youth movement will continue to rebuild the Giants into a winning team. Whether Dave Brown is the answer to Phil Simms remains to be seen. And so far, the Giants have not found a replacement for Lawrence Taylor. Until that time, they will have difficulties reaching the Super Bowl.

But Giants' fans can take heart. The Giants are a club steeped in tradition, a tradition of winning. Because of this winning tradition, Giants fans can expect to see their team atop the NFL once again.

# GLOSSARY

**ALL-PRO**—A player who is voted to the Pro Bowl.

**BACKFIELD**—Players whose position is behind the line of scrimmage.

**CORNERBACK**—Either of two defensive halfbacks stationed a short distance behind the linebackers and relatively near the sidelines.

**DEFENSIVE END**—A defensive player who plays on the end of the line and often next to the defensive tackle.

**DEFENSIVE TACKLE**—A defensive player who plays on the line and between the guard and end.

**ELIGIBLE**—A player who is qualified to be voted into the Hall of Fame.

**END ZONE**—The area on either end of a football field where players score touchdowns.

**EXTRA POINT**—The additional one-point score added after a player makes a touchdown. Teams earn extra points if the placekicker kicks the ball through the uprights of the goalpost, or if an offensive player crosses the goal line with the football before being tackled.

**FIELD GOAL**—A three-point score awarded when a placekicker kicks the ball through the uprights of the goalpost.

**FULLBACK**—An offensive player who often lines up farthest behind the front line.

**FUMBLE**—When a player loses control of the football.

**GUARD**—An offensive lineman who plays between the tackles and center.

**GROUND GAME**—The running game.

**HALFBACK**—An offensive player whose position is behind the line of scrimmage.

**HALFTIME**—The time period between the second and third quarters of a football game.

**INTERCEPTION**—When a defensive player catches a pass from an offensive player.

**KICK RETURNER**—An offensive player who returns kickoffs.

**LINEBACKER**—A defensive player whose position is behind the line of scrimmage.

**LINEMAN**—An offensive or defensive player who plays on the line of scrimmage.

**PASS**—To throw the ball.

**PASS RECEIVER**—An offensive player who runs pass routes and catches passes.

**PLACEKICKER**—An offensive player who kicks extra points and field goals. The placekicker also kicks the ball from a tee to the opponent after his team has scored.

**PLAYOFFS**—The postseason games played amongst the division winners and wild card teams which determines the Super Bowl champion.

**PRO BOWL**—The postseason All-Star game which showcases the NFL's best players.

**PUNT**—To kick the ball to the opponent.

**QUARTER**—One of four 15-minute time periods that makes up a football game.

**QUARTERBACK**—The backfield player who usually calls the signals for the plays.

**REGULAR SEASON**—The games played after the preseason and before the playoffs.

**ROOKIE**—A first-year player.

**RUNNING BACK**—A backfield player who usually runs with the ball.

**RUSH**—To run with the football.

**SACK**—To tackle the quarterback behind the line of scrimmage.

**SAFETY**—A defensive back who plays behind the linemen and linebackers. Also, two points awarded for tackling an offensive player in his own end zone when he's carrying the ball.

**SPECIAL TEAMS**—Squads of football players that perform special tasks (for example, kickoff team and punt-return team).

**SPONSOR**—A person or company that finances a football team.

**SUPER BOWL**—The NFL Championship game played between the AFC champion and the NFC champion.

**T FORMATION**—An offensive formation in which the fullback lines up behind the center and quarterback with one halfback stationed on each side of the fullback.

**TACKLE**—An offensive or defensive lineman who plays between the ends and the guards.

**TAILBACK**—The offensive back farthest from the line of scrimmage.

**TIGHT END**—An offensive lineman who is stationed next to the tackles, and who usually blocks or catches passes.

**TOUCHDOWN**—When one team crosses the goal line of the other team's end zone. A touchdown is worth six points.

**TURNOVER**—To turn the ball over to an opponent either by a fumble, an interception, or on downs.

**UNDERDOG**—The team that is picked to lose the game.

**WIDE RECEIVER**—An offensive player who is stationed relatively close to the sidelines and who usually catches passes.

**WILD CARD**—A team that makes the playoffs without winning its division.

**ZONE PASS DEFENSE**—A pass defense method where defensive backs defend a certain area of the playing field rather than individual pass receivers.

# INDEX

## N

National Football League (NFL)
  4, 7, 8, 14, 17, 20, 21, 23, 24, 28
New Orleans Saints  21
NFC East  21
Nitschke, Ray  17
Nolan, Dick  7
North Carolina University  17
Norwood, Scott  26

## O

offense  14, 20
Owen, Steve  6

## P

Parcells, Bill  15, 17, 20, 23, 24,
  26
Perkins, Ray  14, 15
Pittsburgh Steelers  17
playoffs  14, 21, 23, 24, 27, 28
Polo Grounds  11
Potteiger, Earl  6
Pro Bowl  21, 23, 24

## R

Reasons, Gary  25
Reeves, Dan  27, 28

## S

San Diego Chargers  14
San Francisco 49ers  10, 21, 23,
  24-26
Sherman, Allie  10
Simms, Phil  4, 14, 20, 21, 23, 25-
  28
St. Louis Cardinals  21
Super Bowl  4, 21, 23-26, 28

## T

Taylor, Lawrence  4, 15, 17, 20,
  23, 24, 26-28
Tittle, Y.A.  10, 11
Tunnell, Emlen  4, 6

## U

University of North Carolina  17
University of Southern California
  7

## W

Washington Redskins  11, 21, 23
Webster, Alex  7
wildcard  21

## Y

Yale University  11
Yankee Stadium  8, 11
Young, George  14